D1043611

er

reading. Penguin Young

each Penguin Young Readers
book is assigned a traditional easy-to-read level (1–4) as well as a
Guided Reading Level (A–P). Both of these systems will help you choose
the right book for your child. Please refer to the back of each book
for specific leveling information. Penguin Young Readers features
esteemed authors and illustrators, stories about favorite characters,
fascinating nonfiction, and more!

## Turtle and Snake's Day at the Beach

LEVEL **2**

GUIDED
READING
LEVEL **E**

This book is perfect for a **Progressing Reader** who:
- can figure out unknown words by using picture and context clues;
- can recognize beginning, middle, and ending sounds;
- can make and confirm predictions about what will happen in the text; and
- can distinguish between fiction and nonfiction.

Here are some **activities** you can do during and after reading this book:
- Read between the Lines: You may be able to read the words in this book.
  However, you can get further meaning by looking at the pictures and
  using the text to make guesses (or inferences) about what is happening.
  Use the pictures and the text to discuss and answer the following
  questions.
    - Pages 15–16: What happened to Snake? What does the author
      mean by "wipeout"?
    - Page 17: What happened to the sand castle?
    - Page 32: What prize did the animals win? Why did they win this
      prize?
- Make Connections: Have you ever built a sand castle at the beach? Talk
  about how you made the castle. How long did your sand castle last?

Remember, sharing the love of reading with a child is the best gift
you can give!

—Bonnie Bader, EdM
Penguin Young Readers program

*Penguin Young Readers are leveled by independent reviewers applying the standards developed by Irene Fountas
and Gay Su Pinnell in *Matching Books to Readers: Using Leveled Books in Guided Reading*, Heinemann, 1999.

For Tiggy with love—KS

Penguin Young Readers
Published by the Penguin Group
Penguin Group (USA) Inc., 375 Hudson Street, New York, New York 10014, USA
Penguin Group (Canada), 90 Eglinton Avenue East, Suite 700, Toronto, Ontario M4P 2Y3, Canada
(a division of Pearson Penguin Canada Inc.)
Penguin Books Ltd, 80 Strand, London WC2R 0RL, England
Penguin Ireland, 25 St Stephen's Green, Dublin 2, Ireland (a division of Penguin Books Ltd)
Penguin Group (Australia), 707 Collins Street, Melbourne, Victoria 3008, Australia
(a division of Pearson Australia Group Pty Ltd)
Penguin Books India Pvt Ltd, 11 Community Centre, Panchsheel Park, New Delhi—110 017, India
Penguin Group (NZ), 67 Apollo Drive, Rosedale, Auckland 0632, New Zealand
(a division of Pearson New Zealand Ltd)
Penguin Books (South Africa), Rosebank Office Park, 181 Jan Smuts Avenue,
Parktown North 2193, South Africa
Penguin China, B7 Jiaming Center, 27 East Third Ring Road North,
Chaoyang District, Beijing 100020, China

Penguin Books Ltd, Registered Offices: 80 Strand, London WC2R 0RL, England

The Library of Congress has cataloged the Viking edition
under the following Control Number: 2002153376

ISBN 978-0-14-240157-6          10 9 8 7 6 5 4

PENGUIN YOUNG READERS

LEVEL 2
PROGRESSING READER

# TURTLE AND SNAKE'S
## DAY AT THE BEACH

### by Kate Spohn

Penguin Young Readers
An Imprint of Penguin Group (USA) Inc.

Turtle and Snake are going
to the beach.

They pack towels, an umbrella,

pails and shovels,

and surfboards.

Let's go!

"Look," says Turtle.

"Let's enter the contest,"

says Snake.

Sand Castle
Contest

on the beach
at three o'clock

First, Turtle and Snake

find the perfect spot.

Next, they set up the umbrella
and unpack their beach things.

Then, it's time to start

their sand castle!

They dig, dig, dig.

And they pat, pat, pat.

"It's perfect!" says Turtle.

"I'm hot," says Snake.

"Let's surf!" says Turtle.

Turtle and Snake

ride the waves.

Oh no, Snake.

Watch out!

Wipeout!

Turtle and Snake go back

to their umbrella.

Oh no!

Where did the sand castle go?

Time to build a new sand castle.

They dig, dig, dig.

And they pat, pat, pat.

"It's perfect!" says Snake.

"Let's look for seashells,"

says Turtle.

Turtle and Snake collect

lots of shells.

But when they go back

to their umbrella . . .

Oh no!

Look at that wave!

"Don't worry," says Snake.

"We'll feel better after some

ice cream."

Much better!

Oh no!

Look at the time!

It's almost three o'clock.

"What will we do?" asks Turtle.

"We don't have a sand castle,"

says Snake.

"Don't worry," says Cat.

"We'll all help!"

So they dig, dig, dig.

And they pat, pat, pat.

Will Turtle and Snake

win a prize?

# **Everyone** wins a prize!